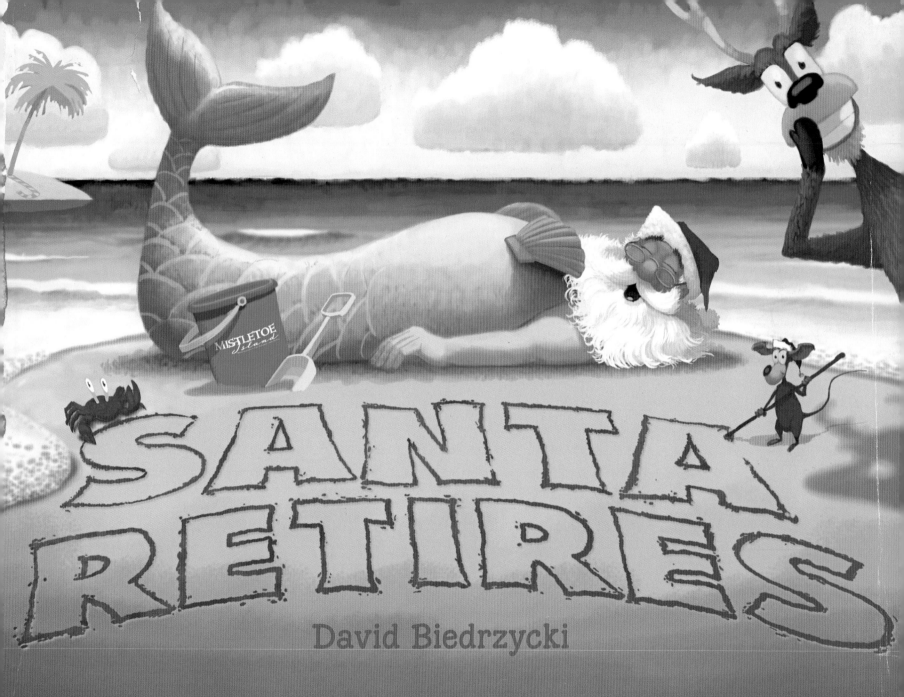

SANTA RETIRES

David Biedrzycki

Charlesbridge

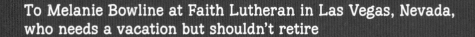

To Melanie Bowline at Faith Lutheran in Las Vegas, Nevada,
who needs a vacation but shouldn't retire

Copyright © 2012 by David Biedrzycki

Published by Charlesbridge
85 Main Street
Watertown, MA 02472
(617) 926-0329
www.charlesbridge.com

Library of Congress Cataloging-in-Publication Data
Biedrzycki, David.
        Santa retires / David Biedrzycki.
            p. cm.
        Summary: Santa Claus is tired of delivering toys and decides
to retire to somewhere warm, but things do not work out as expected.
        ISBN 978-1-58089-293-3 (reinforced for library use)
        ISBN 978-1-58089-294-0 (softcover)
1. Santa Claus—Juvenile fiction. 2. Retirement—Juvenile fiction.
3. Humorous stories. 4. Christmas stories. [1. Santa Claus—Fiction.
2. Retirement—Fiction. 3. Christmas—Fiction. 4. Humorous stories.] I. Title.
PZ7.B4745Sak 2012
813.54—dc23   2011025705

Printed in Singapore
(hc) 10 9 8 7 6 5 4 3 2 1
(sc) 10 9 8 7 6 5 4 3 2 1

Illustrations done in Photoshop
Display type and text type set in Animated Gothic Heavy
    and Hunniwell Bold
Color separations by KHL Chroma Graphics, Singapore
Printed and bound February 2012 by Imago in Singapore
Production supervision by Brian G. Walker
Designed by Diane M. Earley

Just because I wear a red suit and make toys, everyone thinks I'm jolly. Oh, I'm happy when I'm making toys. But when I have to deliver them?

Forget it.
Sacks are getting bigger.
Chimneys are getting smaller.

And you never know what
the weather will throw at you.

Then one day after Christmas, Mrs. Claus
showed me something we got in the mail.

We liked what we saw.

We packed our bags, put the elves in charge, and kissed the reindeer good-bye.

Come to MISTLETOE Island

Where every day is like Christmas, only warmer

Relax
Revive
Retire

Mrs. Claus and I went to the airport and waited in line. We didn't want anyone to recognize us.

I thought we looked pretty cool.

It was hot and sunny when we
arrived at Mistletoe Island.
I was feeling better already.

MISTLETOE
Island

Mr. Tinsel showed us around the place.
He said I reminded him of someone,
but he couldn't remember who.
I couldn't wait to hit the pool.

It had been a long time since
I had been in a swimming pool.

It had been a long time since
I had done a cannon BALLLLLLL!

I needed to lose weight.

So we started playing tennis.
Mrs. Claus was really good.

We did lots of yoga.

We went for long walks on the beach.

I even took dance lessons.

We were eating well and getting in shape. This was the life!
Mrs. Claus and I talked about making Mistletoe Island our new home.

Then the reindeer showed up.
They wanted to party,
but I had a better idea.

I took them surfing.
Rudolph could really hang ten.

But we had to rescue Blitzen.

That night Mrs. Claus served up a healthy meal. I figured it was the perfect time to tell the reindeer I was going to retire.

They didn't take the news very well.

The reindeer sadly went back to the North Pole. Mrs. Claus and I went back to swimming, surfing, and yoga. But things just weren't the same.

I missed my team.

I tried taking a cooking class.
But I wasn't very good at making
a soufflé.

I wasn't very good at tennis, either.
I was good at making toys.

And I just wasn't jolly anymore.

That's when I picked up a newspaper. Things weren't looking good up at the North Pole.

Mrs. Claus and I headed straight for the airport.

When we returned to the North Pole,
we found the reindeer wouldn't eat . . .

toys were missing parts or
had too many parts . . .

and the sleigh had become home
to a family of polar bears.

Mrs. Claus and I rolled up
our sleeves and got to work.

By Christmas Eve the reindeer were ready. So were the toys and the sleigh. It was a beautiful sight.

I was feeling jolly again.

I've decided not to retire just yet. But we did decide to take a vacation every year.

Mistletoe Island, here we come!